Loving Marley

Short or tall,
Big or small;
Feathered or furry,
Don't ever worry.
You're one of our own,
And we'll share our home;
A family together,
Forever and ever!

For our loving companion Marley who
taught us the true meaning of
unconditional love ~ our hearts have bonded to-
gether forever and ever.

and

For Kathy who held our hands the whole way.
Your unwavering commitment,
kind heart and broad shoulders carried all our hopes
and dreams, thank you.

~ Lovingly,
Donald and Sara

Loving Marley

written by

Donald and Sara Hassler

illustrations by

Carol Newsom

PugTale Publishing™

Willimantic, CT

This is a tale about Kurt and Ann Barker and their children Ben and Justy. They live in a home of their own that is filled with love. "I think it's time to share our love," Ann said. Kurt agreed, and they decided to tell Ben and Justy the good news later that day.

"I know we've all been talking about it for a long time, and we think we are all ready—" Kurt explained.

"To get a pet?" Ben and Justy squealed.

"Yes," Ann added. "This weekend we'll go visit Aunt Martha and ask Starlite if we can adopt one of her puppies!"

Ben and Justy cheered.

Over the next few days, they all enjoyed
reading about pet adoption and learning
what it would be like to bring home a new
family member.

On Saturday, Kurt and Ann took Ben and Justy to their Aunt Martha's house.

"Come on in and see Starlite's pups," she greeted. "We've already found good homes for all but one."

"Follow me!" Starlite barked,
leading the way proudly.

"That little one still needs
a home," whispered Starlite,
snuggling her puppies.

For Kurt and Ann, it was
love at first sight.

Ben and Justy wanted
to take the puppy home
right away.

Aunt Martha and Starlite were happy that
they all wanted the puppy. "Adopting a puppy is a
big responsibility," Aunt Martha explained. "Did
you know that loving a pet is a lifelong commitment?
Are all your hearts big enough to love him forever?"

"Oh yes, Aunt Martha, our hearts are big enough to love him for a lifetime!" Kurt and Ann replied.

Then Starlite asked, "Will you promise to keep my baby safe? Will you love and care for him, snuggle and cuddle, feed and play with him every day forever and ever?"

"We promise," Ben and Justy replied.

"Yes, Starlite, we ALL promise," Kurt and Ann added.

"Okay, then," Starlite beamed. "Go home and get ready. Come back and I will be filled with joy to know that my little boy will be going to a loving home."

Kurt and Ann and Ben and Justy left to get ready to bring their new puppy home.

The Barkers decided to name their new
puppy Marley. One day they picked out some
very special homecoming gifts for him.

Over the next few weeks they thought about
Marley every day as they all prepared their
home for him.

Finally the day came for all the puppies to go to
their new homes. Kurt and Ann and Ben and Justy
rushed back to Aunt Martha's house.

Once inside they could all see that
Marley was stronger and bigger.
He was very playful and full of vigor.

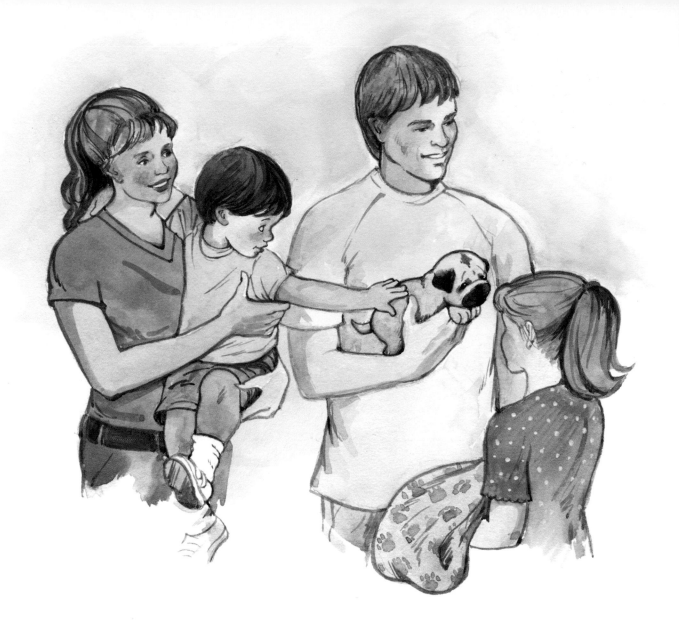

"Oh sweet little Marley, it's time to come home
with us! We'll love you forever!" Kurt and Ann said.
"Yes we will!" Ben and Justy agreed, as they put
Marley into their basket.

But Marley was a little sad. So Starlite bravely said,
"Now off you go, my dear little pup, to a loving family
and home that's all your own forever and ever."

Then Marley was
happy and soon they
were on their way
home to stay.

As they reached their house, Marley could see just how great his new home would be. "Is this all for ME?" he barked happily.

The Barkers
& Marley

As the weeks passed, Marley explored his new home and adjusted to his new family.

Sometimes sharing their love was easy…

...sometimes it was hard.

Something new
happened every day!

At the end of one day, Marley bravely asked,
"Will you always love me and take care of me forever?"
"Of course!" Ben and Justy replied.

Later that night, as Marley drifted off to sleep, Kurt and Ann cooed, "All we want to do is spend our lives loving you."

Short or tall,
Big or small;
Feathered or furry,
Don't ever worry.
You're one of our own,
And we'll share our home;
A family together,
Forever and ever!

PugTale Publishing is dedicated to helping parents and their children understand that pet ownership is a life-long commitment to care for and love an animal. Each PugTale Adventures storybook will delight, teach, and guide young readers and new pet owners as they are introduced to the day-by-day joys and trials that adopting a family pet brings. Commitment, responsibility, and love are the cornerstones of pet ownership and the recipe for a lifetime of fun with our animal companions whether they are feathered, furry or finned.

In *Loving Marley*, the first PugTale Adventures storybook, Marley the pug is introduced. In subsequent titles Belle the pug will join in on the adventures. Marley and Belle are the real-life inspiration for this series of books.

Visit us on the worldwide web at: **www.pugtaleadventures.com** *to learn more.*

Cover design by Alex Fidelibus

Library of Congress Catalog Card Number 2005901620

ISBN-13: 978-0-9766390-7-7
ISBN-10: 0-9766390-7-6

Printed and bound in India
Reinforced Binding

1 2 3 4 5 6 7 8 9 10

First Edition

Published by PugTale Publishing
Willimantic, CT 06226
www.pugtalepublishing.com

Copyright © 2007 by PugTale Publishing

**PugTale Adventures and Marley the Pug
are registered trademarks of PugTale Publishing**

Publisher's Cataloging-in-Publication
    Hassler, Donald.
        Loving Marley / written by Donald and Sara Hassler ;
    illustrations by Carol Newsom.
        p. cm.
        SUMMARY: The Barker family learns that adopting a pet
    is a big responsibility, but that patience and love for
    their new dog will lead to a lifetime of fun adventures.
        Audience: Ages 4-8.
        LCCN 2005901620
        ISBN-13: 978-0-9766390-7-7
        ISBN-10: 0-9766390-7-6

    1. Pug--Juvenile fiction. 2. Family--Juvenile
fiction. 3. Pets--Juvenile fiction. 4. Pug--Fiction.
5. Family life--Fiction. 6. Pets--Fiction. 7. Dogs--
Fiction. I. Hassler, Sara. II. Newsom, Carol, ill.
III. Title.

PZ7.H2789Lov 2007   [E]
        QBI07-600165